Hope You Enjoy!

— W.H. Wax

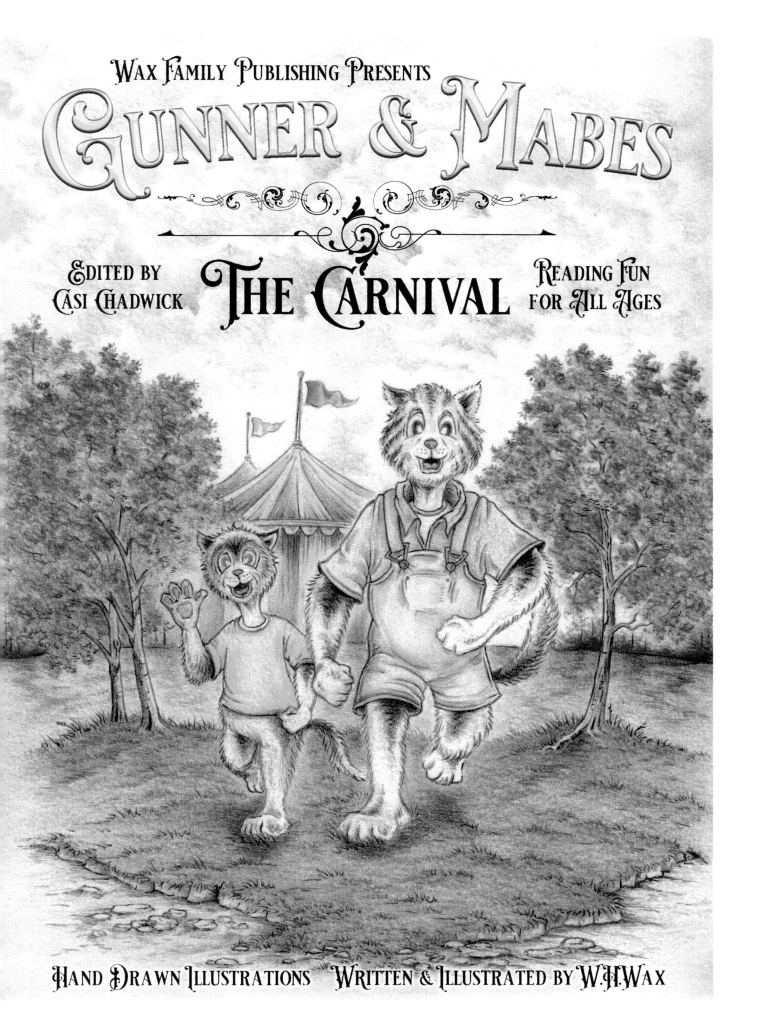

Wax Family Publishing Presents

Gunner & Mabes

The Carnival

Edited by
Casi Chadwick

Reading Fun
For All Ages

Hand Drawn Illustrations   Written & Illustrated by W.H.Wax

Gunner & Mabes
The Carnival

Hand Drawn Illustrations
Written and Illustrated by W.H.Wax
Edited by Casi Chadwick

Published by
www.waxfamilypublishing.com

Copyright © 2021 Wax Family Publishing
Illustrations © 2021 W.H.Wax
www.whwax.com

ISBN 9781098374686

First Edition

Proudly Printed in the United States of America
on SFI Certified Paper

All our dreams can come true,
if we have the courage to pursue them
-Walt Disney

To everyone who believed in me.
Have the courage to believe in yourself and
follow your dreams.
-W.H. Wax

If you're ever traveling through the Ouachita (wash-i-taw)
Mountains of Western Arkansas, near Silver Hill, and you see a
sign that reads "Cooper Road", be sure to come by and visit
Chadwick Acres. It's home to Gunner, one energetic and
mischievous cat, and his very best friend Mabes. It's quite a
special place where you'll meet a whole family of friendly and
interesting animals, who, believe it or not... can talk!

Gunner jumped up on the fence post, startling Ruby and Katie, a couple of sleepy Rhode Island Reds. With all his might, Gunner gives his best impression of a rooster singing, "Ruby, Ruby roo, Katie doodle, doodle, doo, good mornin', good mornin' to you! Howdy ladies! Y'all have a great day, I'm glad ya got to see me!"

With a spring in his step and a happy bounce, Gunner jumped from the fence post and landed on Mr. Jingle's head. "Mornin' Mr. Jingles, how's it goin'?" Mr. Jingle's name is Jerry, they've known each other since Gunner was just a kitten, so to show respect Gunner calls him Mr. Jingles. He's a retired Grand Champion Show Bull that traveled all over the country to some of the biggest livestock and rodeo shows. Mr. Jingles laughs as he replies, "Well, besides you jumpin' on my head nearly every morning, I reckon I'm doin' alright." Gunner replies, "I hear them pigs stirring about, I better go say hello, see ya later Mr. Jingles."

"Good morning Gordie, mornin' Soper! It sure is a beautiful day for wallerin' in the mud!" Gordie astutely replies to Gunner, "We do believe it is ole' boy, we do believe it is!" Gordie is an eccentric bow tie and old straw top hat wearing pig who believes himself to be that of educated swine. He refers to himself as Sir Sus Scrofa Domesticus, that's Latin for domestic pig, but really, he's just an old show pig from Up State New York. Soper, the little guy who looks up to Gordie, well, he's actually the smart one and he's from Oklahoma. He doesn't talk much, he just loves apples. Well, time to move on. There's more stories to tell about these two but that's for another time.

"Mr. Glenn, how are ya? You sure are doin' a great job takin' care of everybody, we sure do appreciate it." Mr. Glenn, he's an ole' cowboy from down around Texarkana, Texas. He's a former World Champion Bullrider and All Around Cowboy who takes care of Chadwick Acres. "Well, thank you Gunner, it's good to see ya this morning. You sure are being awfully sweet, you must want something?" Gunner giggles, "Oh no Mr. Glenn, just sayin' hey." Mr. Glenn replies, "Well, you be sure to behave, ya hear?" Gunner mischievously replies with another giggle, "Oh yes sir Mr. Glenn." Gunner sees Mabes and Jovee up and about, "Gotta go Mr. Glenn, see ya."

"Howdy Jovee! Mabes, whatcha up to?" Jovee is a close friend of Gunner and Mabes, she's a filly that Mr. Glenn had brought up from Texas. "I'm headin' over to see Shilo, y'all wanna come?" Mabes jumps down from Jovee's head to tag along with Gunner. Jovee replies, "Mr. Glenn said he was on his way to saddle me up for a ride, so I'll catch up with y'all in a little bit."

On their way to see Shilo they hear the beautiful and familiar sound of cardinals singing. Gunner runs and leaps up on a branch overhead surprising Adam, the wise old great horned owl and the Songbird Sisters, twin cardinals, Savanna and Sierra Songbird. "Good mornin' ladies! How's it perchin'? Hey Adam, whatcha know good?" Savanna and Sierra giggle, "Goodness! You're so silly Gunner." "Hoo, hoo, good morning Gunner, good morning to you." says Adam.

Gunner jumps from the branch and leans up against Shilo's doghouse, his old friend, a banjo playing Treeing Walker Coonhound, an original Lester Nance Treeing Walker, but that too is another story.

"Hey Shilo, whad'ya say we all go on a real adventure today up around Caney Creek?" Mabes quickly replies with a lump in her throat, "CANEY CREEK! In the Dire Dark Woods?! I don't know guys, y'all know we ain't never allowed to go up in them deep dark woods. There's danger in there ya know!" Shilo replies with his lazy Sunday southern drawl, "Well, whad'ya say we just head on yonder to the Cossatot and see ole' Charlie and Jasper down at the Mize Hole?"

"Hey Charlie, how ya been? Have you seen Jasper?" Charlie, always happy to see Gunner, replies with a welcoming laugh, "Howdy Gunner, it's good to see ya my friend. Ole' Jasper, he's been down the river there all mornin' at the Mize Hole tryin' to catch Jeff, poor Jeff." Jasper is a rather large and intimidating raccoon, but a friendly coon. Jeff, he's a big ole' crawfish or "mudbug" as his cousins down in Louisiana are called. Gunner looks down river and sees Jasper jumping around in the water while Zydeco the squirrel, Christopher the armadillo, and the Turtle Brothers, Terry and Gary Turtle sit and watch in awe.

"Jasper, what on earth are ya doin'?" Jasper replies as if he's annoyed, "Well, ya see Gunner, I been uh studyin' Jeff here for a while now. I been tryin' to catch him all mornin' but he just don't seem to wanna cooperate!" Mabes laughs, "I think it's because Jeff knows you want to eat him!"

Shilo howls and Jovee hops
and gallops with excitement when they
hear a familiar sound, a distant whistle, choo, choo,
chugga, chugga, choo, choo. Shilo continues howling,
"I hear a train a comin'! I think it's the carnival train!" Gunner
shouts with excitement, "Look, it is! It is the carnival train and it's
headed for Silver Hill! Let's go!"

There it is on the edge of town, the carnival! They can't wait to ride the rides, play all the games on midway, and see all the sideshow attractions. There's the world's strongest man, a trapeze artist, maybe even a unicorn, or the scary swamp creature! There's all sorts of interesting, bizarre, and unusual. Oh, and don't forget the animals! Like the circus, this carnival has all kinds of exotic animals, there's a tiger, an elephant, a giraffe, monkeys, and more. After a fun filled day it's time to enjoy their favorite carnival treats! There's yummy kettle corn, candied apples, corn dogs, street corn, and cotton candy!

Everyone's worn out and their bellies are full, but Jovee doesn't want anything to eat. Something must be wrong, carnival food is her favorite. "Hey Jovee, you ok? You're not eating your street corn?" Jovee sobs, "I'm too big for the rides, I can't do anything. Mr. Jingles is a Grand Champion, Mabes is super smart, Shilo can play the banjo, and you're good at everything you do. I'm just Jovee, I'm nothing special." "Jovee, you are amazing, super talented, and you can run faster than anyone! You're the best friend anyone could have!" Gunner does his best to cheer up Jovee, but it doesn't seem to help.

The next day, Gunner makes his rounds as he always does to tell everyone good morning and that's when he soon realizes that Jovee is missing! Where could she be?! Adam, the wise old owl, hears everyone calling for Jovee. He swoops down from his perch to Savanna and Sierra. "Oh dear! Remember ladies, always remember how important it is to not wander off on your own and to always tell someone where you are going! Oh dear, oh dear, I have not seen Jovee, have you?"

The whole cottontail family from Chadwick Warren, Miss Emmy, Billy Tom, Ashley, Tara, Roxie, and Kylee all come running to tell everyone the terrible news and what they just saw. Stumbling over each other's words in excitement and fear they exclaim, "There was this carnival truck you see, and, and it drove away, it did, with Jovee in it! We tried to tell her to never go anywhere with a stranger, but she wouldn't listen!"

With the moonlight to light their way, Gunner and Mabes sneak back into the darkness of the carnival. They peek under a tent to be greeted by a couple of carnival mice.

"Howdy, I'm Amos, and this here is Miss Sherry." Gunner replies, "Hey, we're looking for our friend, Jovee. She's a horse and we think she's been kidnapped!" Amos replies, "Yep, sorry to say, that would be Mr. W.T. Boswell. He's the greedy and wicked old man that owns this carnival. I hate to tell you this, but I know for a fact that he painted your friend white and put a fake unicorn horn on her head. They're forcing her to be in the carnival. Man, it's a crazy circus around here."

Gunner and Mabes quickly crawl under the tent to rescue Jovee when suddenly, a ferocious tiger appears! It's Tye the tiger! Tye springs into action, chasing Gunner and Mabes all around the huge tent! He's running so fast! Tye loses his footing and slides across the straw covered ground knocking over a lantern that quickly starts a massive raging fire! Hugo, the friendly carnival elephant, sees that Gunner and Mabes are trapped in the fire with Tye. Risking his own safety, Hugo charges through the roaring hot flames to save Gunner and Mabes!

Tye sees Hugo coming and he knows he is no match for such an awesome and powerful elephant. Tye jumps the flames and runs in fear. With a graceful but quick swing of his trunk, Hugo loads Gunner and Mabes on his back to rush them to safety. Gunner shouts, "Wait! We gotta save Jovee! She's been kidnapped! They turned her into a unicorn for the carnival show!" Hugo reared up and with a roar says, "Hold on! I know just where she is!"

There's Jovee, just like Amos said, painted white with a unicorn horn on her head. She's locked up behind iron bars in a big dark cage! Hugo loads his trunk with water and sprays it everywhere, extinguishing the fires all around them and soaking Jovee. Hugo rips the cage door open with his powerful trunk! With white paint dripping from her body, Jovee lunges out from the cage! She's free!

Suddenly, to everyone's surprise, Tye is back and he's full of courage, or maybe it's stupidity. While Hugo keeps Tye distracted, Gunner and his friends make a run for the woods in the Ouachita Mountains, the Dire Dark Woods, where they know they should never go! The trees are tall, dark, and spooky, they seem to swallow them up as they sway and creak in the wind. The harsh sound of crows fills the air, caw, caw, caw! The wind makes an eerie howl as it blows through the oak and pine. Moving further into the woods they soon realize that in all the excitement, they are lost!

A piercing sound breaks through the forest! They hear a slow, deep growl and in the glow of the moonlight they see a pair of cold, evil eyes staring down at them from a rock bluff above. It's the legendary evil cougar Cain!

Cain roars and leaps from the rock bluff! Jovee, without pause, bravely stands between Cain and her friends. He viciously attacks Jovee, scratching, biting and snarling! Jovee holds her ground to protect her friends! Rearing up and thrashing at Cain repeatedly with her hooves and teeth, taking one blow after another and returning the same to Cain.

Realizing he has been defeated, Cain quickly disappears into the darkness of the woods. Jovee is exhausted but she stands strong. Gunner and Mabes are amazed, they had never seen this side of Jovee before, this courage and confidence.

Gunner and Mabes shout, "Hooray! Hooray! Jovee is our hero!" "Don't ya see Jovee?" says Gunner. "You don't need to be a Grand Champion or anything like that because you are so much more! You are brave and you have such a big heart! All you gotta do is believe in yourself and just be the best you!" Jovee raises her head, standing so immensely proud she declares, "You know, you're right! If I believe in myself I can achieve anything!"

They continued further into the woods, still lost, for what seemed like hours. Through the strange and creepy sounds of cicadas, tree frogs, and crickets they hear a loud crack and rustling in the woods! OH NO! Could it be Cain again?! Jovee charges ahead with her newfound confindence as she says, "Don't worry, I'll protect you!" Moonlight beams shift in the gentle movement of the clouds and the sway of the trees, breaking brightly through the darkness. Jovee's charge slides to a halt as something magnificent appears before her eyes. It's Lady Casandra! The Mountain Lioness, Queen of the Forest.

"I am so proud of you all. I have watched you from the forest, ready to come to your aide, but you did not need me. I have watched you work together to rescue Jovee, and I watched you, Jovee, as you defeated my evil brother Cain. It is time to go home to your friends and I will show you the way."

Cast & Characters

Gunner - My Grandson
Mabes - Mabey, My Daughter
Jovee - My Daughter
Lady Casandra - Casi, My Wife
Tye the Tiger - My Cousin
Ashley - My Daughter, rabbit in pink
Billy Tom - My Dad and his nickname. Rabbit in green
Miss Emmy - My Granddaughter, rabbit in peach
Roxie - My Daughter, rabbit in purple
Tara - My Daughter, rabbit in turquoise
Kylee - My Daughter, rabbit in grey
Shilo - Our Treeing Walker Coonhound
Mr. Jerry Jingles - Jerry Ermann, Friend - Also inspired by the song "Mr. Bojangles" by Jerry Jeff Walker.
Cain - A Black and Tan Coonhound I had when I was a kid. Also inspired by the story of Cain and Able from the Bible.
Ruby - My Mom, the chicken that Gunner has his arm around
Katie - Our Lester Nance Bred Treeing Walker Coonhound
Adam - My Son
Savanna - My Niece, the cardinal next to Adam.
Sierra - My Niece

Miss Sherry - My Sister
Jeff - My Brother-in-Law
Amos Bagley - My Grandfather
Charlie Wax - My Great Grandfather
Mr. Glenn - Glenn Parsons, Friend
Christopher - Chris Macey, Friend
W. T. Boswell - The initials of my Dad's name and named after Boswell, Oklahoma near where I once lived.
Soper - A town in Oklahoma near where I once lived.
Gordie - Gordie Bice, Friend
Zydeco - A type of Louisiana music that I enjoy.
Terry - My Uncle, The Eastern Box Turtle on the left.
Gary - My Cousin
Jasper - A favorite town of mine near the Buffalo National River in Arkansas.
Hugo - Named after Hugo, Oklahoma where I once lived. A town rich in circus and rodeo history.

Gunner & Mabes

The Carnival

Locations

Chadwick Acres
Inspired by Wax Ranch in Arkansas and named after the Jeff and Kim Chadwick Family

Silver Hill (Gillham)
The name of a town in Southwest Arkansas before it was moved in the late 1800's and renamed Gillham. The Wax Family is also from Gillham.

Cooper Road
Located in Gillham, Arkansas and named after my Great Grandparents, James and Cora Cooper

The Mize Hole
A popular local swimming area on the Cossatot River near Gillham, Arkansas

The Ouachita Mountains
Located in the western portion of Arkansas extending into Oklahoma, the Ouachita Mountains are part of the Ouachita National Forest, the oldest National Forest in the southern United States. Rich Mountain, located near Mena, Arkansas, is the highest peak in the Ouachita Mountains and the second highest in the state at 2,681 feet above sea level.

Caney Creek
Wilderness Area, part of the Ouachita National Forest near Vandervoort, Arkansas where I used to deer hunt and still hike today.

The Cossatot
The Cossatot River, part of the Cossatot River State Park Natural Area near Wickes, Arkansas and the Ouachita National Forest. I grew up swimming, fishing, hunting, and hiking along the Cossatot.

W.H.Wax
Author & Illustrator

W.H.Wax was born in New
Orleans and raised near Doyline,
Louisiana and Wickes, Arkansas.
He is an award-winning artist
who began competing at age 6.
When he is not in his studio
illustrating and sculpting, he is
on the road traveling throughout
the states displaying his artwork
or out enjoying nature.

Casi Chadwick
Editor

Casi Chadwick was born and
raised in Ogden, Utah and is the
mother of four amazing young
ladies. She has built a career in
management and sales. Casi
enjoys spending her time with
family and friends, the outdoors,
and is a devoted mother to her
two Treeing Walker Coonhounds,
Shilo and Katie.

An early illustration of the Gunner and Mabes characters that were not used in the story. The first book in a series, Gunner & Mabes: The Carnival is actually part of a much more in-depth story of all the characters and their adventures. Be sure to look for the next new and exciting book.
Also available are challenging coloring and activity books!

All illustrations are hand drawn with graphite and coloured pencil.

To order go to
waxfamilypublishing.com
whwax.com
or ask for Gunner and Mabes at your local book store.

W.H. Wax working on an illustration

The End

Thank you, we hope
you have enjoyed...

Gunner & Mabes
The Carnival

A concept drawing of Lady Casi